D0408727

White Wolf

Books by the same author

The Fated Sky
Fire, Bed, and Bone

For younger readers

Dimanche Diller
Dimanche Diller in Danger
Dimanche Diller at Sea

White Wolf

HENRIETTA BRANFORD

CANDLEWICK PRESS
CAMBRIDGE, MASSACHUSETTS

The author has created characters and situations consistent with the era portrayed in this book. To accomplish this, the author has occasionally used language which, while not reflecting her personal beliefs, gives the reader an authentic feel for the time and place depicted in the story.

First U.S. edition 1999

Library of Congress Cataloging-in-Publication Data

Branford, Henrietta, date.
White Wolf / Henrietta Branford. —1st U.S. ed.
p. cm.
Summary: A white wolf flees captivity by humans and
must learn to hunt and run with a pack and to discover
what it truly means to be a wolf.
ISBN 0-7636-0748-7
[1. Wolves—Fiction.] I. Title.
PZ10.3.B734Wh 1999
[Fic]—dc21 98-29209

2 4 6 8 10 9 7 5 3 1

Printed in the United States of America

This book was typeset in Plantin.

Candlewick Press
2067 Massachusetts Avenue
Cambridge, Massachusetts 02140

To the tribes of Canada
and to the wolves

Chapter One

A wolf needs water that splashes all summer and turns to ice when the sun goes red. A wolf needs sun on his pelt in the springtime and snow on his snout in the fall. A wolf needs live food with warm blood and running feet.

A wolf needs a pack. All I had was a cage.

How did I get into that cage? Where was my mother? How come my pack left me alone? I didn't know. All I knew was howl and howl some more. Sometimes Jesse would howl with me, putting back his round yellow head and laughing.

I dug until my paws bled and my woolly white fur was dirty, but I couldn't dig out. I snapped at Jesse and his father when they came too close. I sucked up the mush they brought me and snouted for fleas. Even to find a flea would have been something. My ears pricked forward, listening, hoping. But there was nothing to hear and nothing to hope for.

I began to stay in my box all day. I curled up tight and shut my eyes. When Jesse's dad lifted me out, I ran back in. When Jesse put mush down for me, I left it to dry into a crust.

"Eat, Snowy, or Dad'll shoot you!" Jesse yelled. "He'll put a gun against your stupid head and shoot you. He'll sell your skin along with all the rest! Is that what you want, Snowy?"

"If that white cub would grow," Jim said, "he'd keep us safe from here to kingdom come. Indians wouldn't dare harm us with an old white wolf in the yard. But I don't think he's gonna grow."

Jim was afraid of the barefoot people he called Indians. He was afraid of the dark, wet forest where the moss hangs like an old green pelt and the water drips all night. He was afraid of the mountains, where, sometimes, the land slides roaring down into the valleys and the rocks bounce and tumble and other times the fog comes in off the ocean and blinds you. He was afraid of the ocean. He was afraid of most things — not for himself, but for his small son, Jesse.

Jim and Jesse lived alone. Jim was tall with gray hair. Jesse was small with yellow hair. There wasn't anybody else. Jim set traps for animals. I saw him bring them in. Blood dripping. I would run to my box and hide.

Out in the barn lived two evil-minded dogs. Jim called them Devil-You-Know and Devil-You-Don't. They were kept chained during the day but at night they ran loose. Then they'd lie beside my cage, tongues lolling, wicked eyes staring in, whispering horrible things.

Got-No-Mother's looking sorry for himself.

Got-No-Mother's turning into skin and bone.

Why don't you squeeze out under the cage door, Got-No-Mother?

Come out and play with us! We'll teach you games that big dogs play!

Big dogs play catch Got-No-Mother!

And when you catch him, bite him!

I would lie still and quiet in my box, pretending they weren't there. But they knew I knew they were.

One night Devil-You-Know began to dig a tunnel under the wire to get at me. I was afraid, hearing his big paws scrabbling at the earth, smelling his dog breath, listening to him mutter, but he couldn't do it in one night, even taking turns with Devil-You-Don't. In the morning Jesse saw what they'd been up to and ran to tell his father. Devil-You-Know and Devil-You-Don't got a beating and I enjoyed every whack.

Some nights I lay in my box and shut my eyes and breathed deep and slow until there was nothing left of me but the breath drawing in, huffing out. I dreamed about a place where I could run and run and never reach the wire. In my dreams I would lope down an empty valley where a river stood as still as stone. Above, the stars shone brightly. Perhaps, I thought, if I run fast enough, I'll find the great night wolf whose bright eyes twinkle when the sky is dark. If only I could reach him, I thought, I would never wake back in my cage.

Each time I went to the empty valley it hurt more to wake up. When Jim or Jesse brought the rattling bucket I would open one eye, sniff their stink, and tuck my nose back under the soft cream tip of my tail. Jim would make a noise behind his teeth. He would tip out the mush and slop water from a can into my bowl.

"You don't amount to much," he'd say. Or, "Little varmint's fading, Jesse."

One day I dreamed that I had left my thin, white body curled in the cage and was running under silver birch trees in the springtime of the year when a wolf came trotting out of nowhere. He was white like me and his black eyes shone like water. I stopped. He stopped. I crept up to him, tail low, belly to the ground. We sniffed and snuffed each other. I learned that he was free and happy. He learned I was a prisoner and sad.

Until then I had seen no game in the empty valley. But once the white wolf was with me, game was all around us. I could smell a good smell. I could see the flash of hooves and antlers. The white wolf showed me how to work my way around carefully, always downwind of my prey, with its rich smell in my nose. He showed me how to stalk and pounce, to bite down hard and hold, to rip and rend. But each time that I sank my teeth into the rich raw meat, I woke back in my cage, alone and starving, mad with longing for something warm and live to eat.

About that time, Jim began to bring me live food. Chickens, mostly. They pressed themselves up against the side of the cage, reeking of fear while I lay in my box, pretending they weren't there. Jim would shake his head, come into the cage, kill one, and throw it to me warm. I thought of the white wolf in my dreams, and of the good game he devoured. I could not eat what I was given.

"Cub's gonna die," Jim said, one day.

"Don't let him! Do something!" Jesse hollered.

"Maybe I better wring his neck," Jim offered.

But that made Jesse holler more.

Jim went to visit a neighbor. He left before the sun was up and came back in the moonlight. He came back with a small white bitch called Snap at his heel. Snap had two puppies, Sleek and Star, which Jim carried tucked into his pockets. They went away indoors. Jim came back out a while later, picked me up out of my box, and carried me in too. I had never been indoors before. The house smelled of Jim and Jesse, of Snap and her puppies. My own smell was nowhere.

Snap lay in a box full of straw by the fire with Sleek and Star wriggling beside her. Jesse crouched next to them, watching the pups suck. Jim slipped me in beside them and stood back.

"If the little bitch takes to him, that cub might live," he said to Jesse. "If she don't, she'll kill him—and good riddance."

Jesse made a grab to haul me back out of the box, but Jim swung him up and held him tight so he could only watch.

I hunched down small with my muzzle low and my ears back and my tail curved around and down. I did not look up at Snap or her two puppies. I looked away to where Jim's great boots stood on the floor beside the box and Jesse's small foot dangled, kicking.

Snap pushed at me with her nose and snuffed. Her soft ears flopped over her eyes, and her forehead wrinkled as she considered me. I whimpered and she sent me sprawling in the sharp yellow straw. One heavy paw pressed down across my neck, pinning me still. Her muzzle pressed against me, and I felt the nibble of her teeth before her rough pink tongue began to wash me.

"Cub'll do fine now," Jim said, setting Jesse down. Jesse wiped his eyes and leaned his chin on the edge of the box. "Best to leave her be, son," Jim added. "Give her room. She could still turn on him if you worry her." Jesse sighed and crept back to watch from the edge of the rug.

Snap washed me with long, strong licks from my nose to my tail, down, around, and back again. When she had washed me just the right amount for her and a bit too much for me, she let me burrow into her warm flank next to Sleek and Star. I shut my eyes and drew down rich, warm milk.

Star did not seem to mind me. Sleek was angry. He squeaked and butted with his short blunt nose and nipped me with needle teeth. Each time he went for me Snap pulled him gently off by his neck folds and nudged me back to her warm teat. Snap had milk for all of us.

Chapter Two

"Cub's turned a corner," Jim said the next day. Out in the yard Devil-You-Know and Devil-You-Don't complained.

Soft house bitch is feeding Got-No-Mother!

Got-No-Mother's dirty wildwood scum! Leave him alone to starve, house bitch!

Snap ignored them.

When Snap had learned to trust Jesse, she let him lift Sleek, Star, and me out of the box and put us down beside the fire. He laid out little trails of food to tempt us to explore. Sleek and Star would wobble back toward the box and squeak for Snap to fetch them, but I would follow the trail and crunch up anything I found. When I couldn't find any food, I chewed on Jesse's shoe, ripped up the rug, and gnawed the table leg.

Slowly, Star learned to follow if I led. Every

now and then we'd see a flick of gray fur scoot out from the back of the fender and disappear into the sack of skins that lay behind Jim's chair. I did not like those skins. They smelled bad to me, and I would let the gray creature alone once he had reached them. But I watched and plotted, meaning to catch him sometime and investigate his flavor.

We caught him at night when Jim and Jesse were asleep. The fire was low, and Snap and Sleek were curled around each other in the hay box. Star and I were looking for fleas—Star had plenty—when I saw the flick of a gray tail cross the hearth rug. I nudged Star. He slid around to one side of the chair, and I lay in wait on the other. When the mouse crept out from under the skins, four paws landed on top of him. We nipped him in the middle and ate half each. He tasted dusty.

Star and I began to explore the yard whenever Devil-You-Know and Devil-You-Don't were safely chained up. We'd creep out, leaving Snap and Sleek snoozing in their box, to prowl and pounce and practice. We never caught much except spiders, which hardly taste at all, but we were learning all the time.

Sometimes we made Jim angry and he hit us.

When that happened, Jesse would wait until Jim wasn't looking and then feed us tidbits. Often the barefoot people, coming with skins to sell to Jim, would ask to hold or touch me. Sometimes they tried to buy me but Jim wouldn't sell. Once an old man offered a whole bundle of otter skins in exchange for me.

"Otter's good fur," Jim said. "What do you want him for?"

"Big ceremony," the old man said.

"You mean heathen rubbish," Jim scoffed. The old man wouldn't say any more and Jim wouldn't trade.

One evening at dusk, when Jim and Jesse were sitting at their supper, Star and I ran out of the yard and away into the woods. At first we were mad with the adventure of it—night coming, and the two of us out in it alone. The evening smelled of damp earth, leaf mold, bark, and brook. Birds called to one another high above our heads. The wood seemed full of shadows and soft rustles.

Then something grunted just behind us. There was a blast of hot breath, a stink of meat and hair and slaver. We spun around to face a huge hairy rock with wicked eyes and claws like the tines of Jim's hayfork. One slash from them and you'd be finished. It snarled and we saw yellow teeth. We dodged behind a tree trunk. It lurched after us. Stupid with fear, we tried to make a break straight out across the clearing. Bears are fast when they're hungry. He pinned us up against some rocks, and I could see his hot eyes going from me to Star and back again, wondering who to start with. Star yelped with fear. He yelped again and the sound was muffled. I did not take my eyes off the bear but squirmed backward into the crack in the rock that Star had found.

We spent a long time jammed into that crack, with the bear grunting and growling and trying to hook us out with his claws. I don't know if he was hungry or angry. Both, maybe. In the end he lumbered off and left us.

We crouched down, still and quiet, and even when we were sure he'd gone, we did not dare come out. In the end we must have gone to sleep because the next thing I remember was something wet nudging me awake. I tumbled out of that crack in the rock, whining and whimpering, and let the sweet safe smell of Snap comfort me while her brown eyes smiled and her long pink tongue scolded and soothed.

Not long after that, Jesse took me out of the yard and down to the beach, just him and me. I looked back as we ran out of the door and saw

Snap watching with a worried look. Then I forgot about her. Devil-You-Know and Devil-You-Don't were shut in the barn. I heard them talking about what they'd like to do to little house pests. I knew they couldn't get out, so I trotted over and peed against their door.

Jesse and I played all morning. It was a wild, exciting day, with the waves crashing on the shore and now and then long streamers of fog blowing in. Jesse hid behind the rocks. I climbed to the top and yipped down at him. He put me up high where I could not get down. I howled. He lifted me back down. He pelted me with seaweed and I ate it. I ran. He chased. He ran. I hid. Two seals came in, watched us for a while, and swam back out. When we got hungry, Jesse took out his fishing line. He caught three fish and built a fire from driftwood. He ate his fish cooked; I ate mine raw. When we went back to the house, Snap, Star, and Sleek were gone.

I ran to the straw box by the fire. It smelled of them but it was empty now. I yipped and crooned and dug down through the straw. I ran around the room. I searched the yard and put my nose to the crack under the barn door. Devil-You-Know and Devil-You-Don't laughed at me, so I ran up into the woods, not caring about bears. I sniffed and searched and hunted and howled, but they were gone. I stayed all night in the woods, waiting, calling, but they did not answer. In the end, hunger drove me back. I lay down in the house with my nose to the straw box and whimpered.

"Ain't no good crying," Jesse told me. "Dad's took 'em back."

Sometime in the night, alone and miserable, I got inside the box. It smelled of Snap but it was cold and empty. A mouse crept out from behind the fender. He picked up a crumb in his small claw hands and sat up on his haunches. He ate the crumb, then licked his paws and washed his face. Everything he did was quick and nervous, though he did not know that I was watching him. I sat back, still as stone, and watched while he crept nearer to my box. When he was close enough, my jaws snapped shut around his soft, warm body, and I swallowed without biting.

That was my second kill. Nobody saw it but me.

Chapter Three

In the morning Jim caught me before I could go off and search the woods again. He put a leather collar around my neck. He clipped a chain to it and taught me how to run beside Jesse. By beating and reward he made me come when Jesse called and follow where he led me. The lesson lasted many days. When I had learned it and accepted it, which took me a long weary time, Jim took the chain off but he left the collar on. After that he allowed Jesse to go off with me on his own, all day.

"Not too far, mind, nor too fast," Jim said. "He's just a cub still, same as you are. You'll both go bandy-legged if you run too far while your bones are growing. You can go to the head of the creek but don't you go in under the trees. You can go down along the beach but stay out of the water. You can cross the stream but don't go more than a mile beyond."

We went all over the rocky shoreline and up the high ridge behind the house and in under the dark hood of the forest. Everywhere we went I searched for signs of Star and Sleek and Snap—but never found a trace. There was a stream we followed up into the woods. Jesse would fish in the small pools below the waterfalls and I would watch. I caught a fat duck on the water. Above the woods were rocks and wild places. Below, the ocean roared. Sometimes a white wall of fog hid everything, and the trees dripped, and all the noises of the forest sounded louder. Then Jesse would grip my white scruff or slide his hand under my collar, and I would lead him down secret forest trails. Sometimes the barefoot people watched us. Jesse never saw them but I knew they were there.

It was late summer. The grass smelled of sunshine, and there was the good water smell of the stream, and beyond that the moss-and-mist smell of the woods. At first we met no one. But then we were running, chasing a squirrel. Jesse was hot and sweating with that salty savor of his, and I smelled barefoot people. I tried to stop but Jesse dragged me forward. I caught a glimpse of black hair and red-brown skin, earrings of bone and copper. A boy watched us run by, a bundle of red-feathered arrows in his hand. Then we were past, and he was left behind.

That night Devil-You-Know and Devil-You-Don't ran around the yard, peeing on this and that, snapping at nothing, putting on a show of being guard dogs. Jim and Jesse were quiet. Jim had found an arrow by the stream. "Them Indians won't get past the dogs, son," he told Jesse. "Don't you fret."

Jim sat by the window with his gun across his knees and a bottle by his side. I watched from my place by the fire with Jesse beside me throwing sticks into the flames. Presently he laid his head down on my flank, put his arm around my neck, and drifted into sleep. Jim got up and wrapped a blanket around him. He bolted the shutters across the window. He locked the door and sat down by the hearth, with the firelight glinting on the barrel of his gun. He was soon asleep.

Sometime in the night I heard owls hooting that were not owls, and something knocked against the door. Devil-You-Know and Devil-You-Don't growled but they did not leave the yard to see what was going on out in the night. In the morning there was a red-feathered arrow stuck in the door. Jim pulled it out and stood still, turning it over in his large hands, now and then running a finger up against the point. Jesse watched in silence.

"You shouldn't be out here with me, son," Jim said slowly. "Your mom would have had my guts for garters if she knew you was here among the savages."

"Where else can I be?" Jesse asked. "I got to be somewhere, Dad."

"That's just it," Jim agreed. "And you only got me to be with."

After that Jim cut down trees and brought the wood back on a cart he dragged himself. He built a stockade around the house. He strengthened the doors and put thicker shutters on the windows.

I could feel a change coming in the weather. Nights were colder. Days were shorter. Snow fell. Jesse stacked firewood in the yard. He went fishing more often, taking me with him each time. Sometimes he hauled me up into his small canoe, and out we'd go to sea, with sliding green walls of water lurching all around us. I hated that. All the fish Jesse caught were salted down or smoked, filling the house and yard with sharp new smells. Along the edge of the woods Jesse picked berries, and a rich, sweet smell drifted out of the house when he boiled them on the stove.

In the evenings I would stretch myself out beside the fire and let the heat sink in. I knew now that Snap would not come back. But I remembered her smell and her warmth. I wondered where she was and if Sleek and Star were with her still. Outside, more snow fell and water froze. Jesse would curl by my side under a cover made of furs, and we would sleep all night by the embers. I would wake to find my paws touching the still-warm ashes and Jesse, rolled in his cover, pressed against my back.

"Reckon you're the only lad sleeps curled around a wolf," Jim would say. He was proud of Jesse.

"Reckon Snowy's the only wolf sleeps by a fire at night, Dad," Jesse would answer. Jesse was proud of me.

Then came two or three nights when Devil-You-Know and Devil-You-Don't howled and growled and grumbled, and whenever they were quiet, we heard drumming from the barefoot people farther up the coast. One night the drumming stopped. I heard the owls that weren't owls. Then I heard two sharp grunts, followed by silence.

When Jim got up in the morning he found Devil-You-Know and Devil-You-Don't down in the frost and snow with their heads bashed in. A bird that wasn't a bird called from just outside the stockade. Jim slammed the front door shut, shooting home the heavy bolts. He shouted to Jesse to keep back from the window while he fastened the back door and closed the heavy wooden shutters. Jesse crouched beside me with one arm around my neck.

"What is it, Dad?" he whispered. "What's happening?"

"Indians," Jim said. "Heathen savages. They've done for Devil-You-Know and Devil-You-Don't but they won't do for us. I got my gun and you got your wolf. Keep your back to the chimney breast and keep Snowy in front of you. I'll shoot the first damned savage through that door."

Jesse stood with the chimney behind him but I tugged free and ran to jam my nose to the crack under the door. I could smell Devil-You-Know and Devil-You-Don't, and they smelled dead. I smelled the barefoot people and heard the big gate splinter and swing open. I heard whooping and yelling. A rain of thuds shook the door and I jumped back. Then there was nothing. The yard was still and quiet.

For a long time, Jim and Jesse kept quiet too. I sniffed under the door. No one was in the yard. Jim put his gun on the table and sat down, and Jesse ran to him. Jim clamped his arms around the boy, one big hand resting on the top of his small head as if to keep him safe.

"Reckon they've gone, Dad?" Jesse asked.

Jim put his eye to the crack between the shutters.

"Can't see none," he said.

"Will they be back, Dad?"

"Reckon they will, Jesse."

I watched, hungry because no one had fed me, while Jim and Jesse threw things into bundles. Clothes. Food. Ammunition. Jim nailed up the back door and fastened the shutters. Then he set Jesse on his shoulders and swung out of the house into the snowy yard with me at his heels. A strong wind was blowing in from the sea, whirling the snow up off the roof. Jim locked the door and dropped the key into his pocket.

"Where are we going, Dad?" Jesse asked.

"South, to the trading post. I should of took you there long since. Can't go by sea. The wind's too strong and the water's too high. We'll leave the canoe on the beach and go over the mountain. Reckon you'll make it through the snow?"

Jesse nodded. His face was white. His eyes were round with fear.

Devil-You-Know and Devil-You-Don't lay awkwardly in the middle of the yard, snowflakes already hiding their cruel faces. Jesse looked at them quickly, then looked away. The barn door swung on its hinges. Inside, nothing had been touched.

I knew that it was me they wanted.

Chapter Four

Jim glanced around for a few seconds. Then he strode away out of the yard, with Jesse riding high on his shoulders and me trotting beside him.

The path we followed was steep and faint, laid down by pad and paw. It led up the side of the mountain. As we crept inland the crash and thunder of the waves faded, and the woods grew quiet. Sometimes Jesse trotted behind Jim, treading in his father's footprints. Mostly he rode proud on Jim's shoulders. Behind us came the quiet heel and toe of barefoot people. Every time we stopped, they stopped. Jim did not know they were there. Neither did Jesse. Only I knew.

When the sun shone red and the trees cast long black shadows, Jim made a shelter out of brush and branches. He made no fire but fished some cold food out of his bag. He made Jesse eat as much as he could and threw me the rest. It tasted dead, but I ate it because I was hungry.

The forest filled with small night sounds. Snouts pushed under pine needles to suck up what was hiding there. Careless creatures stepped on twigs that cracked. Snow slid from branches, thudding to the ground. Jesse leaned to sleep in the crook of his father's arm. Jim slipped one arm around my neck and sat awake and watchful.

The moon rose, white as a puffball, shone for a while on Jesse's frightened face, and sank behind the mountain. When it had gone, I slept. When I woke up, the barefoot people were close. I put my head down, lifted my lip from my teeth, and growled.

They came in fast around us. Jim pitched forward as I pulled back to spring. I heard the crumple of his clothes as he folded and the thud as he hit the ground. I sat back on my haunches, teeth bared, chest vibrating. Jesse flung his arms around my neck, and the barefoot men drew back and stood still, watching.

Light crept over the rim of the mountain. Jim groaned. Jesse crouched over him, crying quietly. Barefoot men and boys stepped forward and stood in a row, their arrows ready on their bow strings. One of them was the barefoot boy with the red-feathered arrows who'd watched us from beside the stream.

Jesse stood up. He tangled the fingers of one hand into the scruff of my neck. He did not bend down to pick up his father's gun because there were six arrows pointed at his chest.

Two men came closer; the rest stood in a wide circle around us. They kept their bows up and their arrows ready and motioned Jesse to walk. If he had not been holding tight to my neck I think he would have fallen. If he had not been holding tight to my neck I think I would have run.

Jesse looked back at his father, who lay on the ground, not moving, not calling, eyes shut, face clenched like a stone. Some of the men stayed with him. We moved quickly away through the forest, heading north, away from the trading post. Jesse was stumbling, almost falling, tears running from his eyes, snot from his nose, breathing in sobs and gasps.

When he did fall, I stood over him, showing my fangs, daring anyone to come in close. They fanned out around us, squatting, and took dried fish from a bag. They threw us some strips. Jesse didn't want any but I ate all they threw. They smiled and laughed excitedly, reaching out timidly to touch my fur, feeding me until all their fish was gone. The boy held fish in his hand for me, and when I took it, he brushed his hand against my ears. "Careful," the others muttered. But he was not afraid.

When the food was gone we went on. By evening we were over the mountain, and I could smell the sea close by again. Jesse was very tired, walking without seeing anything, one hand gripping my collar. Now and then tears ran down his face. Just before we reached the edge of the trees, a mess of smells hit me—fish oil, dogs, people, smoke—and we came out of the forest onto a narrow, steeply sloping beach with a row of canoes lying side by side along it. Small houses stood along the shore. Carved poles as tall as trees gazed out across the waves.

A longhouse made of cedar wood stood a little way off with its back to the mountains and its face to the sea. It was painted red and black. Carved wolves danced around the door frame, tumbling, rolling, leaping, snapping. They were painted white, like me, and they shone against the dark wood like polished bones.

Dogs barked, someone shouted, people ran out of their houses and stood pointing and laughing, their brown skins gleaming in the red light off the ocean. An old man came forward slowly. His hair was white and stringy, and his black eyes shone out of a maze of wrinkles. He stared at me and smiled and wiped his hand across his forehead.

Jesse had fallen over when we stopped. Now he knelt up, leaning all his weight on me. The old man rested one brown hand on Jesse's yellow hair, stroking a minute, then helped him to his feet. Jesse stared up at him, holding tight to my collar. The old man dropped down onto his knees so that his eyes looked directly into mine.

"My name is Sings-the-Best-Songs," he told me. "I have waited all my life to meet you. I have asked you often, these last years, to visit us. Drums-Louder saw you with the white people. Now, at last, you have come back to us. Welcome, white wolf."

He slipped a leather thong through my collar and led me to the longhouse. Jesse followed, keeping close. Inside, a fire burned. Smoke gushed out through a gap in the ceiling. Everything smelled of smoke and fish and cedar wood. The house was one big room, but behind the fire a wooden screen rose up to the roof, dividing the space in two. It too was carved and painted with a great white wolf that flickered in the firelight. A hole had been cut, like a door, through the wolf's belly.

The old man pushed me through the hole into

the wolf-belly darkness beyond. He tied me to a heavy post. Jesse tumbled through the belly-hole and landed on a pile of blankets. His hands were tied, and he was fastened to the post beside me. He made no noise and I sat very still, watching the hole to see who might be following.

The lad who followed was Drums-Louder, the boy with the red-feathered arrows. He brought us water to drink, and fish—cooked for Jesse, raw for me. We ate and drank. Jesse spilled his water because his hands were tied. Afterward he curled into a blanket and dropped away to sleep still sobbing. He was worn out by fear.

I sat beside him, watching Drums-Louder watching me. Drums-Louder smiled, ate some of Jesse's fish, reached out a hand, and gently pulled my fur, laughing out loud with pleasure. "Is it really you, white grandfather?" he asked. "You are not as big as I had thought you would be. You are about the size of an ordinary wolf. But you're not afraid of people." He shook his head and laughed again. "I'm glad you came to help us. The white people are spoiling our land. You can help us stop them."

Jesse woke up and began to listen. He had learned their talk in Jim's backyard. By and by he asked what had happened to his father and

when he would see him again. His father was dead
and he knew it. But he had to ask. Drums-Louder
shook his head and waved his hand as if to say—
that's not important.

He wasn't interested in Jesse. He was interested
in me.

Chapter Five

Beyond the screen, the longhouse filled with people. I sniffed and snuffed through a crack. Jesse peeped through a knothole. Drums-Louder saw that I was chewing through the leather thong that tied me to the post. He dropped a noose around my jaws so that I couldn't open them. "We can't let you go yet, grandfather," he said. "Don't be angry. There's something powerful that you must do for us first."

The air was fat with good smells. Fish oil in bladder bags hung from the rafters. Dishes of fish oil stood beside each bowl of fish or meat or berries that the barefoot people ate from. Racks of fish dried above the fire. Bears' grease coated the shining, sweating bodies of the people, giving off a rich, strong stink. Sings-the-Best-Songs stood up and looked around.

"People of the Wolf Clan," he began. "We have a visitor from far away."

Everybody nodded. Some of the people hissed behind their teeth.

"Tonight, he will do a big thing for us. First, we will dance for him."

The flames blazed high, flickering on face paint, beads, and knives. Someone began to drum, knocking out slow patterns in the firelight. People began to fidget. One or two began to shake. Jesse leaned close to me, pressing his dirty face into my fur.

People stood up to dance. Some of them sailed like birds. Some swam like fish finning in the current, still and quiet while their world flowed past them. Some danced like deer, delicate and careful, stopping to listen to the drums. One man leapt and spun like a goat, his long hair swinging out behind him. A woman close by screamed and fell against her neighbor. Those around her drummed softly, calling, coaxing. The woman glanced around the hall and up into the darkness of the roof. Suddenly she sat up, shaking, and stared towards the white wolf screen.

When she began to dance, space opened around her. She circled the fire, slow and stealthy, like water running around a rock. The drums beat softly, steadily, like rain. I saw that she was hunting. She listened intently for a few moments to something no one else could hear, then put back her head and howled. I answered her. I could not help myself.

When she had circled the fire, she crept up to the hole in the wolf screen. She leaned in. She smiled at me, narrowing her eyes, keeping her teeth covered. Then she bowed her head and crept back to her place. She sat down, making herself small, and the drums fell silent.

Sings-the-Best-Songs stood up. "People of the Wolf Clan," he began. "Listen to me." They leaned down, comfortable, to listen. "Back in the long-ago, when all things were human beings, the white wolf people at the north end of the world came to visit us." All around the hall people nodded. "They brought a feast with them. But our ancestors would not feast with them. They would not eat or drink or sing or dance.

'Why are you sad?' the white wolf people asked them.

'Because our children grow old, and fall asleep, and after that we cannot wake them,' our ancestors replied.

'All children do that,' said the wolf people. 'This is what you must do. When your children grow old, sing them the song of the white wolf people. That is what we do, and our children return to us as shining cubs each springtime, so that we live forever.'"

Sings-the-Best-Songs shook his head. All around the hall, the people sighed and murmured.

"The white wolf people taught us their song, and we sang it to our children when they slept, and they came back to us, so that we lived forever. But that was long ago. We have forgotten how to sing the white wolf song. Now, when we fall into the sleep of death we do not wake. A few more passing suns will see us here no more. Soon now, the memory of our tribe will be lost, a myth among the white men. I have dreamed what lies ahead for us. It is empty villages and forgotten ceremonial."

No one spoke. The only sound that I could hear was the fire rustling, with now and then a little fall inside it as a branch cracked. That and the small moan of the wind passing over the roof planks on its way north.

"Now, at last, a white wolf from the north end of the world has come to us again. My grandson, Drums-Louder, told me he was here. I will set him free to travel to the spirit world. With my sharp knife I'll set him free to fetch us back his song. Listen! After he's gone, you'll hear his people singing. Listen! Hearing his song, our children who have died will rise and run again. Listen! Hearing his song, our clan will once more be a people of long life. We'll take our land back from the white people because they do not love our country, or know how to live here."

All around the longhouse people sighed.

"Sharpen my knife, Drums-Louder."

Drums-Louder sharpened a knife on a whetstone and the noise was loud in the quiet of the longhouse. He gave it to Sings-the-Best-Songs, who held it up for everyone to see.

Drums-Louder came to me and Jesse. He cut the ropes off Jesse's hands. "Quick," he whispered. "Take the white grandfather out where everyone can see him! Do it!"

Jesse grabbed my collar and tugged but I didn't budge.

"Do it!" Drums-Louder whispered. "Now!"

I had my lips back off my teeth and I was growling. He was afraid to touch me himself.

Jesse was crying. "Please come, Snowy," he whispered. "Please come. I'm sorry, Snowy, but I got to make you." He didn't want to drag me out but he was too afraid to disobey. He pulled a little, gently, on my collar. Still I did not move.

On the far side of the screen someone had

opened up the carcass of a deer. Rich, wet guts flowed out onto the floor, and the good smell of them called me urgently. I had eaten nothing since the dried fish the barefoot people gave me.

I jumped through the hole in the screen and out into the firelight, trotted across to the carcass, and lowered my muzzle toward the belly of the deer. I had forgotten that my jaws were tied.

Sings-the-Best-Songs grabbed my collar in one hand and brought his other hand in under my muzzle. He spoke softly so that only I could hear him. "Taking your life, I set you free to speak directly to your people. With my sharp knife I set you free. Go with our thanks. Bring back the songs to wake our sleeping dead."

Jesse stared up at his lined face, not wanting to believe his eyes. Then he slipped forward, putting both arms around my neck, keeping his body between me and the old man as he tugged desperately at the leather thong around my jaws. Drums-Louder had pulled it tight and I had pulled it tighter, rubbing up and down the post.

Jesse pressed his cheek against my jaws, shut his eyes, and put his small blunt teeth to the leather. He bit down hard but nothing happened. I felt the knife point part my fur, nip at my skin. Jesse's gray eyes flew open and for a second we stared at each other.

Then Sings-the-Best-Songs knocked him flying.

I saw Jesse tumble sideways and leapt at the old man's throat. The weight of my body was enough to knock him over, but with my jaws tied I could not bite him. All around me people were jumping up, grabbing knives, fitting arrows to their bow strings.

"Run, Snowy!" Jesse hollered.

I leapt towards the dark outside the door. I glanced back once over my shoulder and saw Jesse crouched between the painted doorposts of the longhouse, firelight behind him.

Then I ran.

Chapter Six

People ran whooping after me. Arrows flew past on either side of me. Snow fell, cascading off the branches, hitting the ground with a soft thud. An owl called just above my head. Behind me, people yipped and hollered, their voices fading as I pulled away from them. Pine needles silenced my pad-falls, and the cold sharp scent of winter called me up the mountain. Red-brown tree boles stretched back on either side of me. A sighing roof of green flowed overhead. Curtains of trailing moss hung down, glittering with icicles. At the top of the first ridge I looked down.

A trail of sparks blew up into the sky. Along the beach the waves sighed and turned over. Jesse was still down there but I could not go back. I headed inland, running. It was hard to run with my mouth shut, but I did not stop until I had put five ridges between me and the barefoot people, their fire, their longhouse, their strange words, and their sharp knives.

I lifted my head and sniffed the air. The forest was thick and quiet around me. I could smell woods and winter, and now and then a bird. I listened. I could hear the wind in the branches overhead, snow slithering down, and the crack of a twig somewhere. Water splashed close by. It would soon freeze into silence. I was thirsty now as well as hungry. My tracks looked lonely in the snow.

A little more snow flurried down. Frost grew on leaf and twig. Berries that had been red or black turned silver. I tried to eat some but could not because of the leather twisted around my jaws. When the moon dropped behind the mountain and the night grew dark, I crept into a tangle of bushes and slept. I woke often, hungry, thirsty, and afraid, knowing that I could neither eat nor drink nor fight.

When I got up, the day seemed hardly any lighter than the night. Above me, tangled skunkbrush formed a twiggy roof. The leaves had fallen from it; one red flower clung on despite the frost. Above that, dark green spruce and hemlock shut the sky away. Feathers of deep, soft moss hung from the lower branches.

I put my nose down between my paws and scrabbled at the leather. I hooked my claws in underneath the thong. I cut my own nose badly, but I could feel the leather loosening a little as it stretched. Something moved in the moss and leaf mold close beside me. A little, shiny-backed beetle pulled himself out from under a stiff, frosted leaf. It lifted with him and I heard the tiny sound of it settling once more as it dropped back on the forest floor, and the small sound of his legs marching.

I put my nose down next to him and watched. He did not seem to know that I was there. I twisted my neck around to see where he was going and the leather thong snagged on a tree root. I tugged once, sharply, thinking I was trapped, and found that I was free. I leaned out and flipped the shiny-backed beetle into my mouth with the end of my tongue. He was hard and tasted of nothing.

Nosing under the leaf he had crawled out from, I found three more, and under them, a little hoard of grubs. I ate them all, and dug all around but found no more.

I moved out from the skunkbrush and found a little stand of salmonberry. Most of the dark red fruit was gone. I ate what the bears had left, then trotted to the stream. Both sides were frozen solid but there was a narrow thread of water moving in the middle. I drank and drank, quenching my thirst, filling my empty belly up with water.

For the next while I lived miserably on insects and berries. Three times I caught mice, more by luck than stealth. Each one went down faster than the last and none of them helped much. Once I found part of a fish, frozen on the bank of a stream. I swallowed it down. I suppose these scraps kept me alive. I did not know if anyone was following me; I thought perhaps somebody was.

I found a pile of gnawed-down spruce cones, heaped up around the trunk of a tree. It was tall and overgrown with moss. I sniffed at it, finding faint traces of something warm and good to eat. I began to dig down through the cones, slow and careful, and the smell got stronger. My mouth began to water but I dug more slowly and more carefully. I found small tunnels running through the heap and followed one down with my paws and my nose. A squirrel who had been asleep in there jumped out. I killed him with one snick of my sharp teeth and bolted down his small, warm body. There were three more sleeping in the same pile and I caught each one.

After that I investigated each pile of cones I came to. Sometimes a squirrel slept inside and sometimes they were empty. Once I caught a weasel who was doing the same as me, hunting for sleeping squirrels. I ate him too.

Then one day I smelled a white-tailed buck. I smelled fear and sweat and blood on him, put down my head, and began to run. When I slowed, he slowed. When I ran faster, so did he. I moved him on a while, running steadily, until I trotted around the side of a big old tree and found him waiting for me. His shoulder was torn where some other hunter had attacked him. I lowered my head and looked up at him, moving slowly, slowly. He stood still, watching. I moved closer. He shook his horns and bolted. I followed through in a long leap and took him by the throat. I bit and shook and worried till his blood ran down into my mouth.

He was my first big kill. He was weak already from bleeding and he soon fell, or I might not have got him. I opened up his body, took gulping hot mouthfuls, and stuffed my shriveled belly tight. Then I found a warm place in among a twist of tree roots on the bank of a stream. I curled up, heavy and slow from my feast, and slept.

When I woke up it was evening. I lifted my muzzle and sent a long howl to the moon, a sweet, sad wail, falling away at the end into the silence of the forest. I did it again. I cleaned my pelt. I caught a flea. I lifted my leg against the bole of a tree.

Two days after my feast, I found a marten and began to stalk him. The marten, who knew something was up, sat still also, waiting to shoot up the nearest tree trunk as soon as he dared move. He had not seen me but he knew that I was there.

Suddenly, he looked away from me. At the same moment I heard what he had heard. Downwind of both of us a twig cracked. Silence returned but the forest felt different. The marten, sensing a sudden shift between himself and me, fled into the green ceiling.

I pressed my belly to the ground and listened. Slowly, patiently, I crept around through the wood until the wind was in my face instead of at my tail. Fish oil. Wood smoke. Leather. And the sharp smell of Drums-Louder.

I crept away, moving slow and steady until I was sure I'd left him behind. Later that day I passed close by a barefoot village. I heard dogs yapping and saw seal canoes in racks. Fire glowed red through the roof holes of the houses, and their carved poles stood black against the sunset. I thought of Jesse and of Snap. But I did not go down to the shore.

≈

Chapter Seven

≋

That winter I was often cold and always hungry. Sometimes I thought I heard Drums-Louder tracking me but I could not be sure. Once I found a place where someone who smelled of fish oil had been sleeping. There was a shelter made of deer hides rigged over a brushwood frame. A bundle of pelts, fresh and still bloody, hung from a branch. I pulled open a leather bag with my teeth and ate the dried fish that was in it. I chewed the bag and ran off, leaving my big prints in the snow behind me. I headed for an icy stream and ran all night on the smooth ice in the middle, leaving no trail for anyone to follow.

I learned how to shelter deep inside a rock pile while the wind blew and the snow roofed over me, sealing the chinks and shutting out the cold, making a gray and white cave for me to curl inside

and dream the blizzard by. I learned to sniff for
bears in case they'd found the shelter first, and if
their hot stink reached me, to turn and look else-
where.

One evening when the whole forest was whispering in the breeze, I stood still on the edge of a
great fall of rock and looked out across a valley.
Snow was thudding down all around me, and the
streams were babbling. The sun was going down
behind me, and the ground beneath me was
already dark. Only the crimson mountaintops still
caught the red light of the setting sun. I felt
strung-out and restless, alert, and alive to every
falling twig. I had never felt so wide-awake. There
were things I wanted badly but I did not know
what they were.

I put my head back and sent my sad song out
across the valley. Again. Again. When my own
voice had died away, I caught the patter of a barefoot drum from far behind me. I trapped each tiny
message from the evening in the delicate cup of
my large, furred ears and waited. I listened until I
felt the mountain listening with me, until the
valley sucked in its breath and waited, until the air
held nothing but a twanging silence. I called
again. At last the silence peeled apart, and I heard
my own kind answering me.

I listened until there was nothing left of me but listening. My heart was pounding and I was taut and tense from nose to tail with joyful longing. I searched the air for the smell of the pack. Then I was off, trotting fast, splashing through streams, scraping under low branches, scrabbling up and over fallen trees, down into the valley, and up the other side, stopping now and then to call to them, waiting each time to hear their answer.

I smelled their good wolf smell strong in my nose before I saw them. There were four of them, standing together on the flat top of a rock. I heard their little whines and growls. I stood still and stared up at their shining eyes, their rich, thick fur, their listening ears, their soft, red tongues.

Their leader was a big male with dark fur and a dusting of red on his muzzle. Beside him stood a creamy yellow wolf with a dark stipple on her back. They had a yearling between them, pale like his mother, his eyes and ears and mouth outlined in velvet sooty black. Behind him stood a grand-mother with a gray coat and a watchful gaze.

The big male stiff-legged over to me with his tail up in the air and the skin of his muzzle wrin-kled back just enough to let me see his teeth. I drew my ears tight back and down and smiled my eyes to slits. I curled my tail down and around. I made myself as small and humble as I could and waited. The air between us smelled of danger. I drew my tail in tighter and crouched low, turning my head away. Slowly, carefully, respectfully, I brought my nose around till it touched his neck. He knocked me down and bit me. Slowly I eased myself back up. I lifted my head and nudged the corner of his muzzle, pleading. I knew that he might kill me, but nothing could have stopped me from trying to join his pack.

He stared down at me for a short while, then dropped his tail and covered his teeth. His name was Bites-Back, and it suited him. Lick-Up, his mate, knocked me back down at once and bit me hard. Then the yearling made it plain which of us mattered most. I did not argue. Only the grand-mother stood back, watching patiently. There was a lot more sniffing and nuzzling and nipping but I didn't care. If they had not accepted me, I would have followed them anyway, picking up their leavings.

They had killed that day, a mountain goat with yellow wool and long black horns. It must have strayed too far from the high ground, or they never would have caught it. When they revisited the kill, they let me go with them. I ate what they left and chewed the bones and hide. Then we slept a while. I slept as close as I dared to Thin-Moon, the grandmother. Sings-All-Night, the yearling, lay alone, yipping and yowling in his sleep. Bites-Back slept with Lick-Up under a rock a little way away. Once when I woke, I saw him with his muzzle resting on his paws, staring across at me. Thin-Moon got up during the night. She sniffed the wind and trotted away. Bites-Back watched her go but said nothing.

When they were ready to move on, Lick-Up and Bites-Back pushed me over. Bites-Back pinned me to the ground and stared down at me angrily. I lay still until he let me up, then humbly nuzzled him. I greeted Lick-Up politely, nibbling gently at her muzzle, and Thin-Moon too when she returned. Sings-All-Night chased me and tussled with me briefly. Suddenly, everything was settled. I was in.

We scratched and scrambled and sang together. The pale spring sun looked over the rim of the mountain, and a white mist furled up from the valley bottom. All around us moisture dripped from the trees. Winter was over. I was a wolf at last, and life was good.

Each member of the pack knew more than I did about hunting, and each one was my teacher. I was the last to know which way a buck would run, which insect would taste good, which snake was safe to bite, where to cross water, how to find shelter.

I grew sick of lessons. But I fell in love with Lick-Up the first time she washed me. She started with my face, which was muddy. She chewed through the collar Jim had put around my neck and let it fall. Then she checked my paws for prickles and nipped a thorn out of my pad, smiling at me over her sharp teeth as she tugged. If Bites-Back had guessed how I felt about her, young as I was, I dare say he would have ripped my throat out. Lick-Up knew perfectly well how I felt but she kept what she knew to herself.

One morning Lick-Up woke with a new look in her eye. She and Bites-Back went off by themselves, leaving me and Sings-All-Night with Thin-Moon. They were gone for several days. When they came back to us, Lick-Up seemed different. With each kill we made she ate more. She began to run a little more slowly and to stop a little more often, although much of the snow had melted now and the going was easy. Each time we came to a rock fall, or a fallen log, or even just an old fox-hole, she would disappear inside it and root around, digging and snuffing, coming back out at last with earth on her muzzle.

She took the lead, deciding which way we should go, where we should hunt, when we should stop to rest. One morning she led us to the base of a little mountain and began to climb. The place seemed familiar to the others; we followed without arguing. When we grew tired, we lay down in the lee of some rocks with our backs to the stone and slept. When we woke up, Lick-Up had gone.

Bites-Back seemed unconcerned. He found us a little mountain sheep with an injured leg, and we killed it. After we had eaten, he carried off a chunk of the meat. I followed him to see where he would bury it. He headed off up the mountain, and I trotted behind him, keeping out of sight. Presently he came to a tangle of shattered slabs and there he vanished. His scent led in among the rocks and down a narrow chink. It seemed a strange place to bury meat. I pushed along behind him, hoping he would not be angry with me.

The chink turned a sharp corner and opened out into a large, dry hole. Bites-Back was in there. So was Lick-Up. She lay in a dip hollowed out of the soft earth floor. There was a sweet, milky smell about her that I had not smelled before. She put her nose down and pushed gently at something that lay between her forepaws. Two tiny, mewing cubs lifted their faces. Their eyes were shut and their small round ears lay flat against their heads. The bigger cub was dark, like Bites-Back. The little one was gray, like Thin-Moon. Both had little pink tongues the size of leaf tips lolling from miniature black-lipped jaws. Bites-Back nuzzled Lick-Up's face. She snuffed him back. She looked at me and her long elegant ears went back in greeting. She nudged the cubs around to her side to feed, then dropped her muzzle to her paws and closed her eyes.

Lick-Up named the dark cub Thunder-Cloud and the gray one New-Moon. At first she stayed with them constantly and we brought food to the cave for her. When spring was over, she began to leave the den to run and hunt alone. Each time she came back the cubs would feed from her hungrily. Afterward they would chew her ears, or pull her tail, or knock each other down, or play stalk-the-elk and jump-the-water.

By and by Lick-Up decided it was time to leave the fleas behind and move the cubs to a new den. She chose a hollow in the fallen rocks a little higher up the mountain and carried Thunder-Cloud and New-Moon to it. There was not much game, but with five of us hunting we did not starve. We stayed close by the rock den till New-Moon and Thunder-Cloud were strong enough to hunt with us, then moved on.

Now Bites-Back led us and we followed. I no longer ran at the back of the pack. Thunder-Cloud ran behind me, with New-Moon behind him. We hunted deer when we could find them, hidden deep inside the woods. When we could find nothing else we ate berries off the bushes. Gradually, as New-Moon and Thunder-Cloud grew stronger, we jogged for longer times between stops.

One night Bites-Back led us up into high ground, back to a place I knew I'd seen before. He stopped beside a flat shelf of rock, and we stood around him, yipping, nudging, growling. A few white clouds, like belly fur, fluffed around the moon. The valley walls below us glittered. This was the meeting rock, where first I met the pack.

Bites-Back jumped up onto the rock and we saw him silhouetted sharp against the sky as he lifted his muzzle to sing. We hopped up close to him and sang together. Presently, we heard others, answering us.

We sang, *We're here!*

They sang, *We're coming!*

By and by three gray wolves approached, padding long-legged down a ridge. One was old. You could see his bones sliding underneath his pelt, his shoulder blades poking up sharp, his tongue lolling from the long run. The other two were young.

Bites-Back jumped up as they got close, lips back off his teeth, ears forward, tail up, ribs vibrating. The two young wolves hung back while the old grandfather came forward carefully. He was weaker than Bites-Back, lighter, thinner, more worn-out. He put his ears back and smiled, leaving a small kink in his brush to say he'd fight, but only if he had to. Bites-Back swiped him with his own bushy tail, then stood still accepting the old wolf's submission. Lick-Up sniffed him and pushed him with her nose. Thin-Moon merely stood back and looked, as she had done with me. Then it was the turn of the two young ones, whose names were Much and Not-Much. I stayed back till Sings-All-Night had finished with them. Then I bit Much and knocked Not-Much off her feet. Suddenly everyone was nibbling and nuzzling.

When we were ready, we ran off down the north side of the mountain fast and quiet, with Bites-Back out in front. He stopped a long time later and we all stopped behind him. Bites-Back had found elk. We cut a straggler out from the herd and backed him up against a tree stump. His horns were long and branching with points on the ends. When we ran in, he caught Thin-Moon on one horn and tossed her up into the air. She ran with a limp after that. We feasted on that elk for a long time, sleeping and resting between feasts. When there was no meat left on him we chewed his bones and hide and hooves and horns. Then we slept again, curling around each other.

All that winter we hunted and ran and sang in the snow. Day by day, Thin-Moon grew lamer and thinner. One evening, when the first stars showed, she lay down under a rock and called us to her. She was very weak. Lick-Up nuzzled her. Sings-All-Night and I lay down one on each side of her with our ribs pressed against hers, to warm her. Sometimes, when old wolves die, they will tell a story to the pack they leave behind. We waited, silently. Presently Thin-Moon lifted her muzzle and began to tell us the story of winter and spring. Her voice was hardly more than a whimper. We pressed close to hear each word.

There was once an old wolf, she began, who chose a fine place for her den and lined it with leaves. Close by she buried meat to eat when she was hungry. She let no other wolf come in, except only for North Wind, who was her friend. Whenever he was passing, North Wind would visit Old Wolf. He would sit by her fire and smoke a pipe—for wolves enjoyed tobacco, back in the long ago. Now, Old Wolf's fire burned brightly, but it gave no heat.

North Wind had much to do, carrying snow and hail and frost and ice about the world, but when he could, he came, lit a pipe, and sat beside the fire that gave no heat. Old Wolf lay with her paws in the embers but still her whiskers were heavy with icicles and her pelt was silver with frost.

One night as the two friends sat shivering, they noticed a change in the air.

"What warm thing is coming, Old Wolf?" asked North Wind.

Old Wolf didn't know. She didn't care either. Her den felt fine and safe to her.

"Blow off home if you're afraid, North Wind," she laughed.

North Wind blew, and the mountains around about were filled with the snow of his blowing.

By and by came a small knock at Old Wolf's door.

"You can't come in, whoever you are!" cried Old Wolf.

But the small knock knocked again.

"Away with you!" cried Old Wolf.

But the door flew open and into the den jumped a fine young warrior, shaking the snow from his pelt. Old Wolf stared at him. Deep in his eyes she saw the gleam of summer stars.

Old Wolf growled, "My friend North Wind blew out the summer starlight many moons ago. Who are you? Why have you come here, with stars in your eyes?"

The warrior smiled and stretched his paws to the fire. "The Sun is waiting for me to open her door," he said. "She longs to send her broad, strong arrows down onto the earth." He did not tell Old Wolf his name.

Old Wolf began to tremble. "Who are you?" she asked again.

The warrior stood up and shook himself. "My name is Spring," he said. "And yours is Old Wolf Winter. Your time is over now."

Spring Wolf lifted his muzzle to the sky and began to sing the Sun song. By and by a great white bird flew down and picked up Old Wolf Winter in his claws. He flew away north with her and she was gone.

Thin-Moon was quiet for a while, looking at us one by one. She looked longest at her daughter Lick-Up. Then she dropped her gray head down onto the ground. *That is the story of two wolves,* she said. *Their names are Old Wolf Winter and Spring. Now that I have told it to you, you must hunt without me.*

After we lost Thin-Moon, Lick-Up would not eat. She nipped Bites-Back sharply enough to draw blood when he tried to coax her. She snarled at me and Sings-All-Night. She sat apart from us when we were resting, staring back toward the place where we had left Thin-Moon. Sometimes she whimpered in her sleep.

Bites-Back stayed close to Lick-Up always, even though she bit him. He slept pressed against her, groomed her fur, dodged her snaps, comforted her as best he could.

He found places where the grass was tender and where, later on, the deer would feed and grow fat to feed us in their turn. But the deer never came. Instead we smelled barefoot people with their dogs and their campfires, moving onto land that had been ours before.

Lick-Up found a hidden place to be her den but no cubs came to her. If they had, they would have starved. Bites-Back drove Much and Not-Much away to hunt alone as best they might. The old grandfather left with them and I did not see Much or the old wolf again. Perhaps they starved. I do not know. Bites-Back led us back over the mountain.

Chapter Eight

One dusk when we had caught only one cottontail between the four of us and I was chewing part of a hind leg, I heard a noise behind me. I looked over my shoulder and saw Not-Much, standing alone under a tree. Her joints stood out and her pelt was dry and dull. Her ears looked too big for her head. I would have trotted over to her but Bites-Back growled that growl of his and Not-Much ran off.

From then on she followed us, always keeping a few miles between us, picking up anything we left behind—a twist of fur, a bone or two; hardly enough to keep a ghost alive. While the ground was soft enough she could at least eat worms. Worms are all right when you can get them but it takes a lot to fill you up. Once the ground froze, she must have been very hungry. I suppose she killed for herself sometimes, or she would not have survived the hungry time.

One misty dawn I followed Not-Much up into a little wood above a waterfall. It was almost impassable, tangled thick with fallen trees. Not-Much was cleaning her paws when I arrived. She looked up, and hopped neatly behind a tree stump. Sings-All-Night hopped out the other side. I sprang at him and sank my teeth into his neck. He lost his footing and his weight dropped as he went down. I held on, then shook him hard. When I let him go he fell in a tangle of legs and tail and lay snarling up at me. I showed him my teeth and his eyes slid away. I stood back to let him go and he ran.

Not-Much crept out from behind her tree stump and we greeted each other. She showed me where to drink from a little smooth pool that slid off down the valley in a long white fall. We lapped the cold water and sat awhile, contented in the sunshine. Then she trotted off to hunt, and I slept. She came back at dusk with a small fawn and we gorged and slept and gorged again.

That summer we marked out our own hunting ground, just for the two of us. We spent the lazy season taking eggs and chicks and water birds, fish and frogs and snakes around the edges of the lakes. We feasted on slow, fat rabbits. We caught the lambs and kids of wild mountain sheep and goats. We ate the calves of elk and moose when we found them unguarded. Whenever we were hungry we killed—and sometimes when we weren't, just for the skill of it.

I learned every day from Not-Much how a wolf should live. When we were thirsty we lapped cold water from the mountain streams. When we were tired we slept. Whether I woke in the bright moony night, or in the drowse of daytime, Not-Much was close beside me. Soon we knew each other's fleas better than we knew our own.

One day a trapper and his dog crossed our trail. Not-Much sniffed and snuffed. She lifted her head and looked all around with that intent gaze of hers. She bit me and pushed me over on my back to show me that we must take care. Then she led us away into a steep part of the mountain, bringing us around to keep us downwind of the danger.

That night we looked down and saw a small fire flickering red under the tall trees. We smelled smoke and the hot scent of meat cooking and the sharp smell of the spruce someone had cut to make a shelter. A man sat with his back to us, making a little music from a thing he blew into. By and by his dog began to howl.

Not-Much growled and bit me but it was too late. The man by his fire had heard us. He turned to stare up at the mountainside. The red flames of the fire showed me his face, pale in the firelight with a straggling yellow beard. His eyes looked like two black stones in his face.

Next morning early we stood side by side on a cushion of soft green moss, looking away through the trees to where we knew a white-tailed doe and her fawn were feeding. We were alert for danger, reading the morning scents of leaf and grass. Water sang somewhere close by. Far off, a trace of smoke still tainted the air. Closer, the warm flesh of the doe and fawn promised food later.

Not-Much worried a prickle out of her paw and washed between her toes with her tongue. Her face was sand-gold that summer, turning to red over her nose. Her eyes and ears and mouth were edged with black, and a dusting of black fur mixed with the sandy yellow on her back. Her tail was tipped in black, as though she'd dipped it in a mud pool. She looked as strong and healthy as a wolf can look. I snuffed at her neck. She nipped my ear.

A bird called, away up the mountain. It made me feel uneasy. I shook myself and whined. Not-Much led off along the trail. We crossed a stream

and trotted down through woods into a valley
bottom. We came out on a small, green plain
where rabbits nibbled. My stomach tightened at
the thought of food; I was deciding which to go
for when I heard a quiet snick. And Not-Much
screaming.

I ran to her and found her scrabbling at a trap
that held her paw tight in its metal teeth. I dug
down, earth flying back between my legs. The trap
was held by a metal spike driven deep into the
earth. I could not shift it. I licked all around Not-
Much's paw and lay down, pressing close to her to
let her know that I would stay with her. She
pressed back, shaking.

Morning became midday. Not-Much's mouth
lolled open, panting. Her yellow eyes were closed.
We could hear water but we could not reach it.
Her paw, in the trap, was hot and swollen.

Just before dusk we smelled someone coming
through the wood, a white-man smell, mixed in
with tobacco and the trapper smell of skins and
blood. We stood and faced in the direction of the
blood smell, heads down, teeth bared, shoulder to
shoulder. We saw the trapper long before he saw
us. He was walking carelessly, as though the
woods were his. I growled. I would not leave Not-
Much alone to face his knife. He laughed, lifted

his gun, took aim. The sound exploded in my ears. I ran. I could not stop myself. I ran until I realized he had missed me. Then I crept back to see what he would do to Not-Much.

Not-Much was cowering on the path, her paw still held tight in the trap. The white man lay face down with a red-feathered arrow in his back. Drums-Louder stood off under the trees, smiling at me. "Is she your mate, white grandfather?" he asked. "I won't kill her. Sings-the-Best-Songs says that we angered you. He says that we must wait now until you come back of your own free will. If I open the white man's trap and set your mate free, will you come back and help us?"

He picked up a stick and bent over Not-Much, who cowered down, trembling. Slowly he forced the stick between the jagged trap jaws. He leaned on it, forcing it down between the cruel teeth, turning it, prising the jaws apart. Not-Much had her paw out of there and was off all in one second, leaving only a smear of blood and a few hairs in the iron trap.

I looked back only once. I saw Drums-Louder standing beside the empty trap, carefully brushing out all traces of his footprints from the path. Then he turned away, small under the great trees, and set off in the direction of his village.

Chapter Nine

When snow dusted the dark trees silver, we looked for the pack once more. We went first to the meeting rock but found no trace of them. We searched inland but found no sign of any wolves. We turned toward the ocean. Down on the narrow beaches where the orca whales drive up onto the shore, the barefoot people were getting ready for winter. Smoke and sparks rushed up from the roofs of their longhouses. We did not think that we would find the others in among the stink of people, so we ran north, trotting nose to tail, spreading our toes to grip the slippery places, climbing ridge after ridge. We killed when we could and went hungry when we couldn't. At night we shared our warmth, watching the mountains sharpen in the starlight. Not-Much began to lose her summer sleek. Soon I could feel each spine and knuckle of her bones. The trap had lamed her and she was slow to heal.

When spring came around again, Not-Much and I mated for the first time. Sleeping the afternoons away, or in the dark part of the night pressed close against Not-Much's shoulder, I dreamed of the empty valley. I dreamed an endless country, lit by a light I'd never seen. My dreams called me north. But Not-Much had other dreams.

We traveled slowly. She stopped to dig at every empty burrow, peer into each abandoned beaver lodge, examine and explore each hillside, cave, and rock pile.

We stopped one morning, climbed a rocky outcrop, and looked around. To the north was empty space with just a few stands of birch and poplar and some willow here and there. To the south, back where we had come from, the tops of the trees looked as though you could walk on them. Not-Much nosed around while I rested until she found an old fox burrow, its entrance well-hidden by matted, trailing bearberry. Farther down the hill, where a stand of aspen was just turning green for springtime, a trickle of water splashed off down the valley.

The earth was soft and the digging was easy.

Not-Much started to enlarge the burrow. She dug out a bed for us and beyond that, farther into the hillside, a separate small chamber. Then she sent me away. I spent a few days hunting and trotted back up the hill to our den one evening at dusk. I paused at the entrance and looked back down the valley. The smell of rain blew up from the south.

I stuck my nose into the burrow and snuffed Not-Much's good warm smell. Not-Much—and something else. Young, soft, and sweet. Three cubs. Not-Much had licked them free of their small sacks, chewed through each cord, and fed and cleaned each cub. Now they lay sleeping, pillowed against the soft fur of her belly—two little dogs and a bitch.

Not-Much looked up without lifting her muzzle from her forepaws. Her eyes shone in the gloom of the chamber. We touched noses, I nuzzled her face and neck, picking up the slight traces of sweat and blood she had not yet licked off. I cleaned her thoroughly from nose to tail and back again. When she was comfortable I slipped back out to fetch a hare I'd left near by. She nosed it politely but was too tired to eat so I took it back out and buried it for later.

Not-Much slept all night with the cubs, while I lay at the mouth of the den keeping watch. I saw

the stars swing around the sky, heard owls hunting
down the valley, saw the moon rise and set. Now
and then I sang quietly to myself for the joy of
hearing my own voice calling through the large
and lonely space that was my home.

At dawn Not-Much trotted past me on her way
to fetch the hare. We touched noses in greeting,
then she went back to the cubs and I went off to
hunt.

The little bitch pup was the first to open her
eyes. I was washing her face at the time, licking
behind her small flat ears and cleaning her blunt
muzzle. She was trying to push herself up onto her
legs and escape but I held her down gently with
my paw. Not-Much lay beside me with her head
on my flank, watching peacefully. Suddenly she
lifted her nose and yipped softly into my ear. I
looked where she was looking and saw two round
brown eyes peering up at me.

A few days after this, the dog pups followed
suit. One minute they were rolling about between
their mother's paws, butting and nuzzling, eyes
closed, mouths open. The next, they were still:
two small wolf brothers leaned nose to nose and
stared astonished into each other's eyes. Not long
after this their little sharp teeth began to push
through their hard pink gums. They practiced

their chewing skills on whatever they could find—scraps of meat, tatters of hide, my ears, Not-Much's tail.

We named the female first. It was dusk on a springtime evening; Not-Much and I lay curled around each other in our bed, deciding who should leave the den and hunt. We could hear the three cubs in their chamber, squeaking and squabbling, trying out their snarls and grumbles, now and then attempting a pack howl. Then there was a snap and a squeal, and the little female came trotting hesitantly around the corner, climbed over Not-Much and me, and wobbled off toward the mouth of the den. We shifted slightly so that we could watch her.

She stood quiet in the mouth of the den. She had the same delicate ears and shining gray pelt as her mother. Behind her head, high in the soft blue sky, a few stars twinkled. She lifted her small gray head and looked at them. Dusk called her out but danger drove her back. She took a few steps forward, sniffed the air, then scurried back into the den. Stopped. Looked at the world over her shoulder. Trotted toward it and drew back. She took one last glance at the stars, then crept back and lay between us, resting. Not-Much looked down at her and smiled a soft wolf smile. We named her Dances-Along-the-Sky.

We called the smallest male Turn-Over, because he did, each time his brother or his sister pushed him. He was the color of aspen in the fall, a rich, warm, yellow gold. He was the one we worried over; he seemed dreamy, and a wolf is seldom safe enough to dream. The third cub was dark and sleek, like tree bark in the rain—except for a sprinkling of long white hairs over his shoulders and down his back. We called him Frost-in-His-Fur.

All three cubs played and fought constantly, nipping and nudging, stalking and pouncing, chasing, biting, holding. After a night of their squeaking and squabbling, Not-Much would rise and shake herself and trot out into the dawn to hunt, leaving me to guard the den. Frost-in-His-Fur and Turn-Over would venture a short way after her, then turn and race each other back to me. Dances-Along-the-Sky would trot farther and stand in the daylight, ears pricked and listening, wet nose sniffing up the morning news until I picked her up and carried her back inside.

Not-Much never stayed away for long—a day, a night, and she'd be back. We went hungry often, as wolves do, but that spring was a good one. The mountain sheep had their young early and they kept us alive. We meant to stay all summer, growing our cubs. It's what the summer's for.

One afternoon when Not-Much was away and I lay in the entrance to the den watching the cubs play, I smelled smoke. I got up, stretched, and chased the cubs inside. I bit Frost-in-His-Fur to let him know he'd better stay there, and Dances-Along-the-Sky bit Turn-Over, which wasn't strictly necessary. I waited by the den till I was sure they'd stay inside, then went off up the hillside to the top of our ridge. The wind was blowing from the south, and when I turned my face to it, the hot sting of smoke made me sneeze.

I went back down to the den, looking for Not-Much, but she wasn't there. I waited until dusk. It was the longest she had been away from us; the cubs were quarrelsome and hungry. I snapped at them and ran back up the hill. The smoke smell still tainted the breeze; I sat and waited while the land grew dark. A flame began to twinkle on a hillside south of ours.

I ran back down and found Not-Much at the entrance to the den. We snuffed and nuzzled, licking each other's faces, and the cubs came tumbling out to join us, ears back, tails wagging. It was the longest we had ever been apart. Five wolf heads went back. Five wolf muzzles lifted to the moon. Five wolf voices sang the meeting song. The harsh voice of a dog replied.

Not-Much and I stared at each other silently. We huddled up together with the cubs pushed in under our bellies, our noses to the wind. It still blew from south to north. Good. We could smell them. They could not smell us. But the dog had heard us. Maybe the man had too. They had only to get downwind of us to know exactly where we were.

Not-Much had found a bolt hole while she was choosing our den site. She had checked it over briefly and tucked it away in a corner of her memory. Now we ran for it. Not-Much carried Turn-Over, and I took Frost-in-His-Fur. Dances-Along-the-Sky trotted behind.

We ran down the hillside and across the valley, over the next ridge and along beside a stream. We came into a wood of alder trees. We left Dances-Along-the-Sky there, hidden as best we could hide her, because she could run no farther. She curled up tight under a bush and watched us go. Not-Much reached the bolt hole first, dropped Turn-Over, and raced back to fetch Dances-Along-the-Sky. I stayed with the other two cubs in the bolt hole.

Mist bloomed along the river in the valley. The

little sandy hill we'd climbed floated above it, quiet and remote. The bolt hole led into the top of the hill, turning around a bend and opening out into a wide, high cave. The light was dim and soft. The smell was dry, so dry it made us cough.

A low rock ran down one side of the cave and bones lay on it—man bones, long and narrow, and big round head bones, bare and clean. Beads, like the ones the barefoot people wear, were scattered around them, and old unstrung bows and arrows were propped up behind them. Men had lived here, but not for a long time. Claw marks showed where bears had slept the long sleep of winter but no trace of bear smell lingered. Bones of caribou and moose, dry wisps of hide and hair, told me that wolves had lived here too. I pushed the cubs down together at the back of the cave and ran out.

I followed Not-Much's scent back to the place where we had left Dances-Along-the-Sky. Neither of them was there. I called. They didn't answer. Scent on the ground told me which way they'd gone. Dancer had set off first, to follow us. She had tracked us to where we crossed a stream, then lost our scent and wandered upstream. Not-Much had found her scent there. After that the two smells mingled.

Not-Much was following Dancer. I knew I must not leave the other two alone. I ran back to the bolt hole. All through the long, slow day we waited. When at last Not-Much crept back to us she came alone, without our little Dancer. She let the two cubs suckle; then she slept. I nosed her carefully to see if she was injured, found a thorn behind her ear and took it out, then sat in the cave entrance a while. There was no smell of enemies. No man, no dog. By and by I stole out.

First I went back to where we had left Dances-Along-the-Sky. Her scent was fainter now, but still present, overlaid by her mother's scent for some way. Their trails led out of the wood and down a boggy valley. There Not-Much's trail turned off and headed back toward the cave.

Dances-Along-the-Sky had trotted deeper into the bog. I followed for a little way, then lost her trail. I cast in a wide circle but found nothing. On my third circle I found a whisper of scent and followed it to the edge of a lake. Beavers had dammed the stream at one end and an empty lodge, falling to bits now, still blocked the end of the pool. The scent trail led into the water. Farther along the bank I smelled lynx. Perhaps, seeing a lone cub, it had chased her. Perhaps she only smelled it, and was frightened. She must have run into the water.

I lay down on the bank of the pool with my head on my forepaws. Time passed. I lifted my face to the sky and let a whimper go as quietly as I could. Another followed it and then another—small, quiet breaths carrying my sadness. All that night I lay alone on the wet ground. When the sky lightened I stood up and shook myself. I stared across the water, yellow now from the rising sun. I drank a little. I howled because I couldn't hold my howling in.

Quietly, with the high quaver of a young wolf, Dances-Along-the-Sky howled back across the water. I splashed into the pool and swam, joyful and careless of the danger, sending a spray of cold clear water up around my paws. I hauled myself, panting, on to the wreckage of the beavers' lodge. Dances-Along-the-Sky was limp and damp and shivering with cold, but before I could shake the pond water from my pelt she was nipping and nuzzling, squeaking, dancing, rejoicing that her fear and loneliness were over. I picked her up gently, holding but not hurting her with my long, curved teeth, and carried her back to Not-Much and her brothers.

We danced the welcome dance together, piled ourselves into a wolf heap, snuggled and nuzzled her, petted and pushed and played, chased fleas, chewed ears, wagged tails. We checked Dancer for cuts and thorns and swellings, found none, and did it all again just for the joy of it.

Late that night I went alone to sit on a rock and sing my pleasure to the sky wolves. That was foolish of me. It brought the trapper man. I smelled his dirty skin-and-blood smell, a smell like no other, slaver and wood smoke and meat, man and animal all mixed up. I barked a warning down toward the bolt hole, then circled around, careful as only a wolf can be, keeping downwind of the man until I found a rocky place where I could look down on him from a distance.

This is what I saw.

A little fire. Orange flames. Wood glowing red. Smoke blowing up and away. Beside the fire a shelter made of branches. Between the shelter and the fire the man sat cleaning his knife. Presently he untied a sack and pulled out a bundle of soft gray pelts. Wolf pelts. He scraped at one and then another with his knife. Worked on them a while. Smoothed them out, rolled them up, and put them back in the sack. He leaned into the shelter and pulled out a tangle of traps. I saw their sharp iron teeth in the firelight and thought of Not-Much, her paw hot and swollen, her face tight with pain.

The man checked his traps, oiled them, then wrapped them in a roll of leather and put them by the sack. He put a pot over the fire and from out of the pouch, and from his pockets, and from a box he carried in his knapsack, he took a pinch of one thing and a handful of another, a scrape of this and some drops of that, and a slice cut from something else. One by one he dropped them in the pot, and sniffed, and stirred, and smiled. Pretty soon a good rich smell drifted up to me where I lay watching. A sweet smell, a tempting smell, a smell that said *eat me*.

The man stood up, tugged part of a white-tailed buck down out of the branches of a tree and cut it into biggish pieces. Carefully, with his sharp knife, he cut into each piece of meat. Then he scraped something out of his pot with a stick and poked it into each cut. When he had finished, he dropped the pieces into a sack and hung them back in the tree. He lifted the pot off the fire, using the sleeve of his jacket to keep his hand from burning. When he threw the stick on the fire it burned up blue and then green. After that the man went into the shelter, and soon I heard him snoring. Then all was quiet for a while.

I ran back to the bolt hole. Not-Much was waiting for me, the cubs asleep in a warm tangle
behind her. Frost-in-His-Fur and Turn-Over
looked fine but Dancer shivered and whimpered
in her sleep. She didn't look as though she would
be strong enough to run with us just yet. Safer to
stay a little while, we thought, and hope that neither man nor dog would find us.

All the next day I watched as the man laid out
his traps and baits. He must have left his dog tied
up because I heard howling now and then. The
sound made my blood race. Toward evening the
man went back to his camp. I ran off to hunt then,
running north, away from them. I got nothing—
all the game had been scared off—and returned
hungry to the den where Not-Much waited, even
hungrier, having fed the cubs.

I lay in the mouth of the hole, studying the air
and listening. That's when I smelled them
coming. I smelled dog first. Then man. Then dog
again. A sweet smell this time. Why sweet? I had
no time to wonder why. The dog caught our scent
and leapt ahead, running toward us, head down,
yipping and yahooing.

I drew my weight back onto my haunches,
opened my jaws a fraction, and lifted my lip back

all along my teeth. Behind me Not-Much scooped up Turn-Over. I knew I must kill the dog quickly. There must be no struggle. The man must walk by, hearing and seeing nothing. Go for the throat. Find the windpipe. Bite. Grip. Clench. The dog must suffocate in silence.

Not-Much shivered. Dances-Along-the-Sky whimpered once, softly. Then the cave darkened and filled with dog smell, and my jaws stretched wide. I took hold hard on the invader's neck and with one twist of my shoulders lugged the beast inside the den. I took a lung full of the creature's smell, ready to choke it into limp defeat.

Instead of danger, I smelled comfort. Instead of fear, love. Snap's wrinkled face gazed up at mine in disbelief. Silent in the darkness of the den we pressed against each other, nosing, nudging, snuffing, tails swinging stealthily in spite of danger outside. Behind us Not-Much crouched, bewildered.

The man came up with his second dog on a chain. If the dog smelled us—and he would smell us—we'd be finished. The man would kill us. A squirrel—one mouthful of brainless fluff—saved all of us. It skittered down out of a tree and ran across in front of the dog, who yipped and yapped and tugged at his chain until the trapper laughed and let him go. The dog was off. The trapper shrugged and followed, whistling Snap back to his heel. Snap turned to go. I nuzzled her. Dancer whimpered. Next minute, Not-Much and I grabbed one cub each and fled. Snap ran beside us, nudging Dancer along as we dashed down to the stream and down the far bank to the pool, choosing boggy ground that wouldn't hold our scent.

By dusk we were holed up again five valleys to the north, this time inside the base of a big old hollow tree beside fast-running water. When we had rested, Not-Much killed two ducks. I got a beaver that had strayed too far from the water. Snap found a nest full of eggs and ate those. We were all alive, and all safe. But Not-Much would not let Snap inside the hollow tree or near the cubs. She did not trust her. Snap had to sleep under the shelter of a rock.

Snap could track well enough, and her stalk was not bad, but she did not have the strength to kill anything big. Still, she seemed able to feed herself, and tried her best to feed the cubs as well. Each time she brought in fur or feather she would pad with it proudly to the hollow tree and drop it on the ground. She would call softly to the cubs and out they'd tumble, sharp teeth and pink tongues dripping hunger. Snap always tried to stay close while they ate, but Not-Much would not let her. She drove her back to watch from a distance while the cubs devoured her gift.

Dances-Along-the-Sky ignored Not-Much's fears and took to Snap at once. Whenever Not-Much was away from the hollow tree, the two of them would lie close, washing each other or just watching from some high point the last of the caribou going north to calve in the bare lands.

The cubs were not old enough to hunt with us yet. Not-Much would not leave them in Snap's care, nor would she hunt with Snap, so all three of us hunted alone. When we were tired, Not-Much and I curled around the cubs inside the hollow tree and slept in a tight knot. Snap slept alone outside.

Once, when I woke, I saw that Dances-Along-the-Sky had woken before me and crept out. She and Snap lay beside the stream, and Snap was washing her, carefully, gently, just as she had washed me long ago. She was concentrating on the cub and did not see me watching. But I saw her look of deep contentment and was glad.

≋

Chapter Ten

≋

We stayed at the hollow tree until the cubs were strong enough to travel. Then we took off, back to the bolt hole. Snap found life hard. One afternoon I woke to see her drag in, panting, still with a smear of blood across her muzzle from the kill, and drop down, whining quietly. I went to her. She was tugging at one of her forepaws. I nosed it gently, licking between her toes, working carefully around her claws, searching her tough old pads to find the site of the damage. Part of a porcupine quill had snapped off in her paw, and the tip was deeply embedded. The broken shaft was still near enough the surface but I couldn't get it out without causing her pain. She wouldn't let me try.

All that day she lay and nursed her paw, growling at me if I came close. At dusk Not-Much and I went off to hunt. When we got back, Snap was still lying where we'd left her, worrying at her paw. I caught the sick smell of infection. A dog with an infected paw can't hunt and what can't hunt can't live. Not-Much stiff-legged across to Snap and growled down at her. Sometimes we kill our own when they are sick or injured. I waited to see what she would do. She wrinkled her nose and bared her teeth and barked an angry challenge. Snap dragged herself up onto her feet, ears back, tail down. She held her injured paw clear of the ground. Not-Much shoved Snap once, hard, with her nose, and sent the old dog sprawling. I looked away.

Suddenly, Dances-Along-the-Sky was there, running in between Not-Much's bared teeth and Snap's proffered neck, yipping softly. She pressed her snout to Snap's injured paw, sniffing and worrying at it, seeking out the source of the infection. Not-Much drew back. Snap lay still. Dances-Along-the-Sky twisted her little head this way and that, probing Snap's swollen paw unmercifully until she caught the stump of the broken quill in her sharp teeth. Then she put her head back and her paws forward and pulled. Snap yelped once and out it came—a tiny piece of quill. After that Not-Much let Snap into the pack and life was easier for all of us.

Snow thickened and we ran single file. There was a lot of darkness. Now and then the sun swam over the brow of the land, paused a while, then sank like an old wolf settling into sleep. The fish and the beavers disappeared under the ice. The squirrels burrowed down, curled tight, and slept. Our pelts grew thick and heavy. Even Snap grew a warm layer of fur under her shaggy coat. Not-Much gleamed like feathers and my own white pelt kept out the coldest weather. Who knows at the start of winter if they will see the spring? And yet, I love the winter.

It was that year the raven joined us. We had noticed one following us when we began to follow caribou. It seemed to know where we were going before we did. When we lost the caribou in a ground blizzard, Turn-Over decided that we should follow the raven once the storm had died down. It led us back to the herd. We did not kill that day, nor the next, because the snow was piled too high to run through. But we stayed with the herd, and on the third day we killed a cow. We were a little weak by then and she fought hard. The snow was red all around her by the time we brought her down.

Her meat was warm and there was plenty of it. We tore and swallowed till our bellies were tight.

Then we strolled over to the shelter of a tree with low green branches sweeping the snow. We dug a hollow underneath, lay down belly to back and nose to tail and rested. We cleaned one another's faces and nuzzled for fleas. Frost-in-His-Fur had a splinter of bone in his lip. Dances-Along-the-Sky pulled it out for him. Not-Much nibbled my ear. I swatted her with my bushy white tail. We were content. We shut our eyes. We dozed.

When I woke up, Turn-Over had left the warm huddle and was sitting beside the kill, chewing a piece of fat. Up in a tree the raven perched. I closed my eyes and dozed again. Next time I looked, the raven was down in the red snow, tearing morsels from the carcass. Beside him sat Turn-Over, still chewing. Neither took any notice of the other until both had finished eating. Then Turn-Over turned his back on the raven and began to wash himself. The raven hopped over and pecked his tail. Turn-Over spun around and snapped at the bird. It lifted clear of Turn-Over's teeth, flapped a couple of times, and landed on the other side of him.

Dances-Along-the-Sky was watching too, and presently she trotted over to join in. The three of them hopped and snapped, teasing one another, until the rest of us got up and took a little more meat off the carcass. The raven pecked up some red snow and flew up into his tree to watch us.

After that he fed from all our kills. If we could not find caribou, we'd send Turn-Over up to some high place to look out for the raven. We'd go in his direction, and often we'd find the caribou close by. Sometimes we could not find the raven, but it never seemed to happen that he failed to find us.

The nights were shorter now, and we slept out on the hillside. It was good to feel the sun on our spring pelts, to watch the lazy swirl of the river below, where now and then a bear came to fish, to sleep and wake, and to read what news the wind brought to our noses.

One dusk, when the sun had dipped down yellow and shadow drowned the land, I sat up on Snap's rock, listening. Dances-Along-the-Sky sat close by with her sharp ears pricked. The mist rose off the water and spilled over the valley until our hilltop seemed to rise and float free. Everything was still. You could hear a fish rise in the river below. Not-Much slept safe in the den. Snap lay below, invisible beneath a curtain of green.

For no reason that I knew, I began to feel afraid. I whined softly. Dances-Along-the-Sky whined back. Her wise little face looked troubled and uneasy. We stood up and turned our heads into the soft night breeze, drawing scent and sound toward us.

They were a long way off. Barefoot people, singing the hunting song. It is a good song when you're the singer but not so good when you're the prey. They were running fast. When they stopped singing, I knew they must be running faster. They had no dogs with them, or we'd have heard them barking. I was not really worried. Without dogs to lead them they'd never stumble on our den.

Dances-Along-the-Sky hopped down to the mouth of the den. I listened for a moment longer, tasted the wind, and followed her. Snap and the others were inside. I pushed Not-Much softly with my nose. Then I went and sat in the entrance to the den and looked out over the valley. A thin moon looked over the hill and pearled the sea of mist. There was no sound except now and then the yipping and yelling of the barefoot hunters. All other hunters—owl, bear, and wolverine—were waiting.

The breeze shifted around and brought me their scent though I could not yet smell what it was they hunted. Soon I could hear their feet—or maybe I could feel them—drumming on the ground. Splashing now and then when they crossed water. Panting. They made no other sound.

Suddenly one set of running feet separated out in my mind. One smell. One sound. One of them was ahead. The rest behind. They were hunting one of their own.

Their prey began to stumble up the hill. The rest, behind him in the valley, paused, turned, and followed. I backed into the den. Not-Much crept up and stood by my side, head down, teeth bared. We could smell and hear somebody swinging up the hillside. A cracked twig here. A rustle there. I could not see him yet but I knew who he was.

He stopped, blowing a little, at the foot of our mound. Cloud shifted off the moon, and the sand of our digging shone pale. Next minute the young man was down on his hands and knees, crawling into the tunnel. I could hear his heart thudding and smell his fear. He was dazed with running and did not see us at first but he sensed us. He looked around the cave and saw our eyes shining in the darkness, and his fear became terror. His hunters were close now, loping and leaping up the hill, grunting and yipping with excitement. He could not run. He could not stay. He curled over with his face against his knees and rocked. I crept up quietly and pushed my nose against his ear. He shrank back. I nudged in under his protecting arm and licked his face. Jesse.

The hunters put their heads back, yelling while their leader dropped down and crawled part way into the tunnel. His face was dark but I could see the paint on his skin. Jesse scrabbled up onto the rock shelf, sending white bones rattling and rolling out across the floor. There was a dry *chink chink* as one of the round head bones rolled down the tunnel. It rolled right up to the barefoot leader and came to rest close to his face. His scream crashed around the den; then he was gone.

Behind me Jesse sat up and opened his eyes. He saw me, white in the moonlight, and stared. He shook his head slowly. "Snowy?" he whispered. "That you, Snowy?"

Snap crept out of the back of the cave and licked his face. "Old Snap? You there?" She licked him again, her tail wagging. "You two just saved my life. Those men wanted me dead. They reckon I'm a thief. Maybe I am. I thought there was game enough for all." He stared into the dark cave and shook his head again. "Dad? You there too?" He peered around, half afraid, then stood to stare back down the hill.

The hunters were scrambling back down, silent and fearful. When they stopped at the bottom and

looked back they saw Jesse standing in the moonlight with a round head bone in his hand and a
great white wolf at his side. They ran.

That night Jesse slept once more with his arm
around my neck. Snap lay close by with her head
under his hand. Not-Much and the others stayed
at the back of the cave, fearful and bewildered. At
dawn, Jesse sat up and rubbed his eyes. He saw
me and smiled. He patted Snap. Then he looked
around and saw four big wolves watching him. He
crawled out of the cave, moving slow and steady.
He stumbled down to the bottom of the hill and
sat with his back to a rock, his gun across his
knees, breathing slow and careful. Snap followed
and lay down at his feet, but I hopped up onto the
high rock and watched him from there.

Jesse made a camp down by the river and fed
himself by fishing. Not-Much and I looked down
at dusk or dawn and saw him sitting lonely by his
fire. Sometimes he made music. Sometimes he
sang. Often he looked toward our den as though
he wished that he could be with us. Once, when
we were howling up a hunt, he put his head back
and howled with us, just as he had when we were
both younger.

Snap could not bear to see him by his little fire
at night, alone, or tramping home alone at dusk

with what small game he'd killed. She began by visiting him, but she was soon his dog and visited us. Her joints were stiff; her teeth were worn. I think she knew she could not hunt with us for long. One season, maybe two. Meanwhile, I longed for the empty valley.

Dark days and colder nights returned. The caribou flowed south with their yearling calves. All of us wintered well. Jesse and Snap hunted hard and killed many, eating the meat and using the hides for warmth and shelter. I would lie in the mouth of the den with my back to the wind and watch out of the corner of my eye the glow from Jesse's camp. His shelter was low and white and rounded now with snow. As winter deepened there came a time of ground blizzards, days and nights when Jesse could not step outside to hunt. Once he came stumbling right up to the den and dug up some of our cached meat.

On the first clear day, when the wind dropped and the snow lay flat and hard all the way down the hill and out across the frozen river, Jesse stamped out his fire, put his gun over his shoulder, and whistled Snap to his heel.

Snap trotted in his footprints for a little way,

then turned and trotted back toward me. I was
watching from up on her old rock. She stood looking up a while, ears pricked, tail low, whining. I
hopped down off the rock and ran to her. I looked
into her soft brown eyes and licked a snowflake off
her muzzle. Then I held still for her to wash me
one last time.

By and by Jesse stretched his hand out to me,
and I walked toward him, slowly. Jesse had been
my companion when I was a cub. Jesse could sing
like a wolf. I leaned my muzzle in his hand. He
knelt in the snow and smoothed my coat from
nose to tail. He laid his cheek against my face. For
a few moments we looked into each other's eyes,
just as we had in the longhouse when Sings-the-
Best-Songs had his knife at my throat. Then he
stood up and called Snap to him.

Jesse slipped a leash through Snap's old collar. I
watched as the two of them went away through
the snow that fell now, white on white, like goose
feathers. For a little while their tracks led back to
Jesse's shelter by the river. Then the snow drifted
over them and they vanished, sinking into winter,
and we never saw them anymore.

I put my muzzle up to the sky and sang out to
tell the others it was time to leave. Dances-Along-
the-Sky came first. Then Turn-Over, his yellow

tail waving, yipping now and then to tell Frost-in-His-Fur to hurry. Not-Much came last. She chirped and swished her gray tail. She looked at me impatiently. It was time to go.

A NOTE FROM THE AUTHOR

"A few more passing suns will see us here no more"—these were the words of Chief Plenty Coups of the Crow Indians. His speech begins: "The ground on which we stand is sacred ground. It is the dust and blood of our ancestors."

The Crow people did not live on the coast, like Sings-the-Best-Songs and Drums-Louder and the people of the Wolf Clan, but I have lent Chief Plenty Coups's words to Sings-the-Best-Songs because they are more beautiful and more apt than any I can invent.

For the same reason I have lent him some of Chief Seattle's words as well. It was Chief Seattle who spoke about the memory of his tribe becoming a myth among the white men.

For the rest of it, I've tried to take a little from several of the peoples of the northwest coast—Kwakiutl, Haida, Nuu-chah-nulth, and others. I cannot claim to know enough about their rich heritage to have drawn them, any of them, accurately. In any case, this is a work of fiction. But it is dedicated to them, and to the wolves whose hunting prowess they respected and admired.